Northfield Public Library
210 Washington Street
Northfield, MN 55057

1421322
J 796.48 Ma
$19.95

INDEX

Belmondo, Stefania, 20
Bjørgen, Marit, 20
Bjørndalen, Ole Einar, 14
Bolt, Usain, 5

Colledge, Cecilia, 18
Comăneci, Nadia, 11

Gerevich, Aladár, 8
Grafström, Gillis, 9
Griffith-Joyner, Florence, 12

Heiden, Eric, 16
Hirscher, Marcel, 17

Jones, Jennifer, 19

Kim, Yuna, 21
Kim Yun-Mi, 18

Latynina, Larysa, 10
Lawes, Kaitlyn, 19

Matt, Mario, 17
McEwen, Dawn, 19
Millar, Ian, 6

Officer, Jill, 19

Phelps, Michael, 4, 10

Rothenburger-Luding, Christa, 13

Selanne, Teemu, 17
Smetanina, Raisa, 20
Swahn, Oscar, 7

Thorpe, Jim, 7,

Zöggeler, Armin, 15

ABOUT THE AUTHOR

Tyler Mason studied journalism at the University of Wisconsin. He has covered professional and college sports in Minneapolis and St. Paul, Minnesota, since 2009. Tyler and his wife live in Hudson, Wisconsin.

TO LEARN MORE

IN THE LIBRARY

Herzog, Brad. *G is for Gold Medal: An Olympics Alphabet*. New York: AV2 By Weigl, 2015.

Peters, Stephanie True. *Great Moments in the Summer Olympics*. New York: Little, Brown and Co., 2012.

Stewart, Mark. *Olympics*. Pleasantville, NY: Gareth Stevens Publishing, 2009.

ON THE WEB

Visit our Web site for links about the Olympics: **childsworld.com/links**

Note to Parents, Teachers, and Librarians: We routinely verify our Web links to make sure they are safe and active sites. So encourage your readers to check them out!

GLOSSARY

biathlon (bye-ATH-lon): The biathlon is a sport in which participants carry a rifle as they ski on a course and stop to shoot at targets along the way. Ole Einar Bjørndalen was a great champion in biathlon.

curling (CUR-ling): Curling is a sport played on ice in which two teams slide stones toward a target at the other end of the ice. Canada's women's curling team went undefeated in the 2014 Olympics.

decathlon (di-KATH-lon): The decathlon is a track-and-field contest consisting of 10 different events. Jim Thorpe won the decathlon at the 1912 Olympics.

equestrian (i-KWESS-tree-uhn): The equestrian competition is a horseback riding event. Canada's Ian Millar competed in the equestrian events at 10 Olympic Games.

fencing (FEN-sing): Fencing is a sport in which swords are used to score points. Aladár Gerevich won a fencing medal in six straight Olympic Games.

luge (LOOZH): The luge is a sport in which one or two people race down a track on a sled. Armin Zöggeler medaled six times in the luge.

pentathlon (pen-TATH-lon): The pentathlon is a track-and-field competition made up of five events. Jim Thorpe also won the pentathlon at the 1912 Olympics.

sprinter (SPRIN-tur): A sprinter is an athlete who runs fast over short distances. Usain Bolt is one of the world's fastest sprinters.

uneven bars (uhn-EE-vuhn BARZ): The uneven bars are a women's gymnastics event that uses two bars set to different heights. Nadia Cománeci scored a perfect 10 on the uneven bars in 1976.

BEST FIGURE SKATING SCORE
228.56 Points
Yuna Kim, 2010

South Korean Yuna Kim made her mark at the 2010 Games in Vancouver, Canada. She posted 78.50 points in her short program, easily taking first place into the free skate. Then she blew away the rest of the field with a score of 150.06. The second-place skater scored 131.72. Kim's two-round total of 228.56 was a record. She added a silver medal to her collection four years later in Sochi.

YUNA KIM

MARIT BJØRGEN

MOST TOTAL MEDALS
10 Medals
Raisa Smetanina, Stefania Belmondo, and Marit Bjørgen

Three cross-country skiers are tied atop the all-time women's winter medal standings. Raisa Smetanina of the Soviet Union, Stefania Belmondo of Italy, and Marit Bjørgen of Norway each have won 10 medals. Bjørgen won three gold medals in the 2014 Sochi Games. She could set a new record if she medals at the 2018 Games in PyeongChang, South Korea. She will be 37 years old at the time.

FIRST UNDEFEATED CURLING TEAM
Canada
2014

No women's **curling** team had won all of its matches in one Olympic Games until 2014. The Canadian team was a perfect 11-0. Jennifer Jones was the skip—or captain—of the squad. Kaitlyn Lawes, Jill Officer, and Dawn McEwen also competed for Canada. They beat Sweden 6-3 in the gold medal match.

CHAPTER 4

WOMEN'S WINTER RECORDS

YOUNGEST OLYMPIAN
11 Years, 73 Days Old
Cecilia Colledge, 1932

In the 1932 Games in Lake Placid, British figure skater Cecilia Colledge made history. She was just 11 years and 73 days old when she took the ice. Colledge finished eighth that year. She came back for the 1936 Games in Garmisch-Partenkirchen, Germany. That year she won a silver medal. Kim Yun-Mi is the youngest medalist. The South Korean speed skater won a gold medal at the 1994 Lillehammer Games. She was 13 years and 85 days old.

MOST CAREER HOCKEY POINTS
43 Points
Teemu Selanne

Teemu Selanne played hockey in six Winter Olympics. He helped Finland win medals in four of them. At age 43, Selanne scored twice in the bronze medal game in the 2014 Sochi Games. That set the record for most career points (goals plus assists) in the Olympics. Selanne also played 21 seasons in the National Hockey League (NHL). He was among the top 15 in career NHL points when he retired.

SO MANY SKIERS

The Sochi Games in 2014 featured athletes from 89 countries. A record 61 athletes competed in one event—men's slalom skiing. Austrian Mario Matt won the gold medal. His countryman Marcel Hirscher won silver.

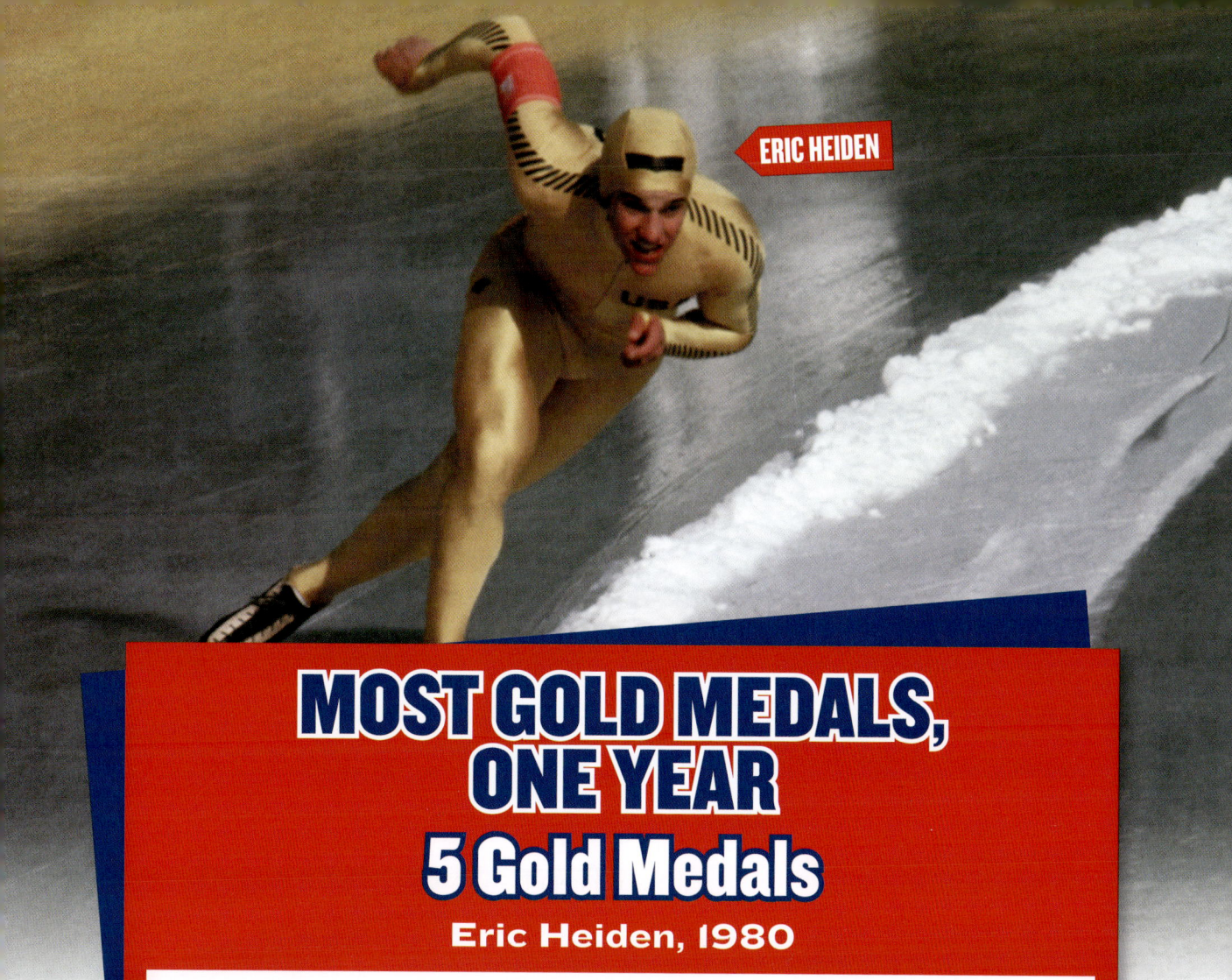

ERIC HEIDEN

MOST GOLD MEDALS, ONE YEAR
5 Gold Medals
Eric Heiden, 1980

Eric Heiden represented the United States in speed skating at two Olympics. In 1976 the 17-year-old came home empty-handed from Innsbruck, Austria. Heiden did not win a medal that year. But he made up for it in 1980. The Olympics that year were held in Lake Placid, New York. Heiden did not just win. He set Olympic records in all five of his events. His time in the 10,000-meter race was a world record at the time.

MOST OLYMPIC GAMES WITH A MEDAL
6 Olympic Games
Armin Zöggeler

Armin Zöggeler of Italy had a good run in the **luge**. Zöggeler won medals in six Winter Olympics. His first medal was a bronze in men's singles at the 1994 Games in Lillehammer. He finished in the top three in that event for the next five Olympic Games. Zöggeler won the first of his two gold medals in 2002 at the Salt Lake City Games. He also won gold in Turin, Italy, in 2006. In 2014, at age 40, he brought home a bronze medal from Sochi.

ARMIN ZÖGGELER

CHAPTER 3

MEN'S WINTER RECORDS

MOST TOTAL MEDALS
13
Ole Einar Bjørndalen

Norway's Ole Einar Bjørndalen competed in **biathlon** in six straight Winter Games. He began his Olympic career in 1994 at age 20. He was shut out that year in front of the home crowds of Lillehammer, Norway. But Bjørndalen was just getting started. He won a gold and a silver at the 1998 Games in Nagano, Japan. Four years later, he raked in four gold medals in Salt Lake City, Utah. He also won two gold medals at the 2014 Games in Sochi, Russia, at age 40. That made him the oldest individual gold medal winner in Winter Olympic history.

ONLY SUMMER/WINTER MEDALIST, SAME YEAR
Christa Rothenburger-Luding, 1988

Christa Rothenburger-Luding of East Germany set a record that can't be broken. In 1988 she won gold and silver medals in speed skating at the Winter Games in Calgary, Canada. Seven months later, Rothenburger-Luding took silver in cycling at the Summer Games in Seoul. The Summer and Winter Games are no longer held in the same year, so Rothenburger-Luding's record is safe.

CROWDED FIELD

A record number of athletes competed in the 2008 Summer Games in Beijing. A total of 10,901 athletes participated. That broke the previous record of 10,648, which was set in the 2000 Summer Games in Sydney.

FLORENCE GRIFFITH JOYNER

FASTEST 100-METER DASH
10.62 seconds
Florence Griffith Joyner, 1988

The 100-meter dash is one of the most exciting events in track and field. No woman was better at it than Florence Griffith Joyner. The U.S. sprinter set a world record in 1988. She ran the 100 in 10.49 seconds at an Olympic trial race. She then set an Olympic record with a time of 10.62 seconds in Seoul, South Korea. Griffith Joyner also set another record that year. She ran the 200-meter dash in 21.34 seconds. Both times were still records going into the Rio de Janeiro Games in 2016.

FIRST PERFECT 10
Nadia Comăneci, 1976

For years, a perfect score in gymnastics was 10.0. Nadia Comăneci was the first to earn a 10.0 in Olympic competition. The 14-year-old from Romania charmed the crowd and judges at the 1976 Games in Montreal, Canada. She won three gold medals that year, shining on the balance beam and in the all-around competition. But she made history in the **uneven bars** competition, where she scored her perfect 10.0.

NADIA COMĂNECI

CHAPTER 2

WOMEN'S SUMMER RECORDS

MOST INDIVIDUAL MEDALS
14 Medals
Larysa Latynina

Gymnast Larysa Latynina competed for the Soviet Union from 1956 to 1964. In three Olympic Games she won 18 medals. Fourteen of those were individual medals, which is a record. No Olympian has won more individual medals. U.S. swimmer Michael Phelps had won 13 individual medals through the 2012 London Games. Half of Latynina's 18 medals were gold. She also won five silver and four bronze medals.

FIRST SUMMER/WINTER MEDALIST
Gillis Grafström
1920 and 1924

Several athletes have won medals in both the Summer and Winter Olympics. Gillis Grafström from Sweden was the first to do it. What's odd is that he won gold in the same event. Figure skating began as a Summer Olympics competition. Grafström won the gold medal in men's singles at the 1920 Antwerp Games. Four years later he won gold again. But this time it was in the first Winter Games in Chamonix, France.

GILLIS GRAFSTRÖM

ALADÁR GEREVICH

LONGEST MEDAL STREAK, SAME EVENT

6 Olympic Games
Aladár Gerevich, 1932–1960

Aladár Gerevich represented Hungary in **fencing**. His first Olympic competition came in the 1932 Games in Los Angeles. He won the gold medal in men's sabre. He won individual or team medals in the next five Olympics. His final appearance was at the 1960 Games in Rome, Italy. There were no Olympics in 1940 or 1944 due to wartime restrictions. Gerevich is the only Olympian to medal in the same event six times. He retired with 10 total medals, seven of them gold.

OLDEST OLYMPIAN
72 Years, 281 Days Old
Oscar Swahn, 1920

Oscar Swahn was from Sweden. He competed in shooting. In the 1920 Summer Games in Antwerp, Belgium, he set a record. He was 72 years and 281 days old. No Olympic competitor has ever been older. Swahn won a silver medal that year. He finished his career with six medals. Three of them were gold.

Jim Thorpe is considered by some to be the greatest athlete of all time. He won gold medals for the United States in the **pentathlon** and the **decathlon** in the 1912 Summer Games in Stockholm, Sweden. Eight years later, the National Football League (NFL) began. Thorpe played for the Canton Bulldogs in 1920. He played in the NFL until 1928, when he was 40 years old. Thorpe was a trailblazer of sorts. More than 40 Olympians have played in the NFL, but he was the first.

IAN MILLAR

MOST OLYMPIC APPEARANCES
10 Olympics
Ian Millar, 1972–2012

Most Olympians compete in just one Olympic Games. A fortunate few represent their countries more than once. Ian Millar competed for Canada in 10 Olympic Games. He first entered the **equestrian** events at the 1972 Games in Munich, West Germany. He was 25 years old. Over the next 40 years Millar competed in every Summer Games except one. Canada boycotted the Olympics in 1980. Despite his numerous chances, Millar brought home only one medal. He won a silver medal in 2008. But his story is a reminder that being able to compete is a victory in itself.

FASTEST 100-METER DASH
9.63 Seconds
Usain Bolt, 2012

People call Usain Bolt the fastest man alive—with good reason. Bolt is a **sprinter** from Jamaica. He ran the 100-meter dash faster than any other Olympian at the London Games in 2012. But even that time was not a personal best. Bolt ran the 100 in 9.58 seconds at the 2009 world championship. That broke his own record. He had run it in 9.69 seconds in the 2008 Beijing Games.

CHAPTER 1

MEN'S SUMMER RECORDS

MOST GOLD MEDALS, ONE YEAR

8 Gold Medals

Michael Phelps, 2008

U.S. swimmer Michael Phelps has earned his way to the medal stand more times than any other Olympian. In the 2008 Games in Beijing, China, Phelps was unstoppable. He won five individual gold medals and broke the world record in four of those races. Phelps added three more gold medals—and three more world records—as part of U.S. relay teams. Four years earlier in Athens, Greece, Phelps medaled in the same eight races. Six of those medals were gold and two were bronze.

CHAPTER 1
Men's Summer Records...4

CHAPTER 2
Women's Summer Records...10

CHAPTER 3
Men's Winter Records...14

CHAPTER 4
Women's Winter Records...18

GLOSSARY...22

TO LEARN MORE...23

INDEX...24

ABOUT THE AUTHOR...24

Published by The Child's World®
1980 Lookout Drive • Mankato, MN 56003-1705
800-599-READ • www.childsworld.com

Acknowledgments
The Child's World®: Mary Swensen, Publishing Director
Red Line Editorial: Editorial direction and production
The Design Lab: Design

Photographs ©: iStockphoto/Thinkstock, cover, 1, 2, 23; Andrew Cowie/4156-4156-6/ Colorsport/Corbis, 5; Jochen Lübke/DPA/Corbis, 6; Press Association/AP Images, 8; ullstein bild/Getty Images, 9; Suzanne Vlamis/AP Images, 11; Durand; Giansanti; Perrin/Sygma/Corbis, 12; Tobias Hase/EPA/Corbis, 15; Bettmann/Corbis, 16; Sun Media/Splash News/Corbis, 19; Filip Singer/EPA/Corbis, 20; Andrew Mills/Star Ledger/ Corbis, 21

Design Elements: Shutterstock Images

Copyright © 2017 by The Child's World®
All rights reserved. No part of this book may be reproduced or utilized in any form or by any means without written permission from the publisher.

ISBN 9781503808904
LCCN 2015958451

Printed in the United States of America
Mankato, MN
June, 2016
PA02307

INCREDIBLE OLYMPIC RECORDS

BY TYLER MASON